French Adventures

Part 2

written by Jeremy Strong
illustrated by Amanda Wood

Chapter One

Alone in Paris

The trip to France was not turning out as expected. Mouse and Sam stood at the street corner. They could hardly believe what had happened. Mr Hopkins had been kidnapped, and now they were lost in the middle of Paris. They could not speak French.

All around them people hurried past. Cars swooshed by. The air was filled with the noise of car horns and engines, shouting and busy footsteps.

Sam pulled Mouse into the shelter of a doorway.

"What are we going to do?" moaned Mouse.

Sam bit her lip. She was not at all sure. There was so much to think about. Should they try and do something about Mr Hopkins? "We can't look for Mr Hopkins," she told Mouse. "We have no idea where he's been taken."

"But why would anyone want to kidnap Mr Hopkins?" wailed Mouse. "It doesn't make sense!"

"I know," said Sam. "I'm scared. I think the best thing we can do is get back to the church. I'm sure the rest of the school won't go without us. They will notice that we are missing, and then they'll wait for us."

Mouse was almost jumping up and down. "But don't you see, Sam? Mr Hopkins has gone too. Everyone will think that we are with Mr Hopkins. They'll probably think we have gone back to the coach or something."

"In that case we must find the church before they go," said Sam. "Come on."

Mouse and Sam hurried back they way they had come. They reached a corner. Should they go right, or left, or straight on?

"Did we cross this road?" Sam asked.

"I don't know!" wailed Mouse.

"I remember that shop," Sam said, and she pulled Mouse down the next street. They half ran and half stumbled. They dodged between the crowds. "Let's try down here," cried Sam.

On and on they went, but there was no sign of the church. At last Sam stopped. She looked at her watch. “We’ve been gone for at least an hour,” she said. “Miss Cherry will be tearing out her hair by now.”

“*If* she’s still waiting at the church,” Mouse pointed out gloomily. “She may have called the police. We are in so much trouble. We’re in big trouble, if they ever find us.”

“Look, we can’t find the church,” said Sam. “We shall have to go for Plan Number Two.”

“But what is Plan Number Two?” Mouse asked.

Sam fished inside her T-shirt and pulled out her name and address card. “Mr Hopkins said we should use this in an emergency.” Sam looked at the faces of the people hurrying past. How could she just go up to one of them and show them the card? Who should she choose? Suppose she chose someone nasty, or unkind?

Mouse was gazing into the window of a shop. It was a bookshop, and there was something that puzzled Mouse. He turned to Sam. “Why are all these books in English?” he asked. “We’re in France. They should be French books, not English.”

Sam looked at the display. Mouse was right. All the books were English. She gazed up at the sign above the shop. “It’s called Shakespeare,” murmured Sam. “He was English. Maybe they speak English inside. Come on.”

Sam pushed open the door. It was quiet inside the shop. Two or three people were looking at books. There was a smell of paper and dust.

A young woman was sitting behind the counter, reading to herself. Mouse and Sam went across to her. Sam took a deep breath. “Excuse me, but do you speak English?”

"Of course I do, honey!" the woman answered in a strong American accent, and she smiled at the two children. "How can I help you?"

Sam was filled with relief. But as she opened her mouth to answer, her eyes suddenly filled with tears. Instead of saying anything she burst into sobs.

Everyone in the shop stopped and stared at Sam and Mouse.

Chapter Two

Meeting Montana

It was the shock. It was too much for Sam. She was just so pleased to be able to talk about what had happened.

The woman's name was Montana. She gave Sam a huge hug. She found some tissues and wiped Sam's eyes. Now that Sam had stopped crying the customers went back to looking at the books.

"Now then," said Montana. "Tell me what this is all about."

Mouse began to tell their story. Montana raised her eyebrows further and further. Her mouth fell open. Her eyes grew round. At one point she suddenly reached out and stopped Mouse in the middle of a sentence. "You're not making this up, honey, are you?"

"Of course not!" shouted Mouse.

"Okay, okay. It's just that it's ... Gee, I mean, it's like a film!"

Mouse finished the story, with a bit of help from Sam. Montana called over one of the shop assistants. She said that the children had a problem. "Can you look after the shop for a short time?" she asked the assistant. "I'm going to take Sam and Mouse to the Church of Saint Germain to see if their school group is still there. If they are, that's fine. If they're not I shall bring them back here and we'll have to call the police."

"We'll be in terrible trouble," whispered Mouse.

Montana ruffled Mouse's hair and smiled. "Don't worry. I won't let anyone be cross with you!" Montana took them out of the shop and they made their way back towards the Church of Saint Germain.

"I've got a secret to tell you," Montana said. "When I was twelve I ran away from home. After I had left I realised that what I wanted to do most of all was to go back home. I was scared and I was tired and hungry. I wanted to go home, but I was very afraid. I thought my mum would be cross with me. I thought she would shout and scream and then I'd be even more unhappy."

Mouse looked up at her. "What happened?"

"Well," said Montana, "it started to get dark and cold. I decided I would have to go back home, so I did. My mum was so pleased to see me! She wasn't cross. She was happy that I was back safe and sound. That's what will happen with you two. We will get you back with your friends and your teachers, and everyone will be happy that you are safe and sound."

"It's true," Sam said quietly. She was remembering the time she had run away from home.

By this time they had reached the church. Montana was holding each of them by the hand and they ran up the steps together. They hurried into the dark body of the church.

It did not take them long to realise that the rest of the school had gone. Montana gave her glasses a quick polish while she thought about what to do next.

"Okay, back to the shop. We'll telephone the police and you can tell them about your teacher, Mr ...? What was his name again?"

"Hopkins," Sam said.

"Yeah, Hopkins. And we'll telephone the place where you are staying so that they know you are all right. Then we can organise some way of getting you all back together again. Hey, that Hopkins guy – clever man! That was a neat idea to give you all cards with telephone numbers and stuff. The only thing is, he's the one who's lost!"

Mouse and Sam grinned at each other. Maybe they still had lots of problems, but Montana made them feel safe and comfortable.

Chapter Three

Up the Eiffel Tower

On the way back to the bookshop Montana bought some cakes from a bakery. "These are the best cakes in Paris," she told Sam and Mouse. She took them through to a back room in the bookshop.

"This place is more like a house than a shop," said Mouse. There were big armchairs amongst the book shelves. People could sit in them to read. In the back room there were two beds.

"Sometimes people stay overnight," said Montana. "We have had lots of well-known writers staying here."

"Has Zak Pieman ever been here?" asked Sam.

Montana shook her head. "He writes books for children, doesn't he? No, he hasn't been here. Most of our books are for adults. Now, sit down here and try some of this cake. I have already phoned the police and they will be here soon."

Montana saw the worried look on Sam's face, and on Mouse's too. She smiled. "Don't worry. It will be all right, I promise. Anyhow, I shall stay with you. Come on, eat up."

The cakes were just as wonderful as Montana had promised. All three of them were still brushing crumbs from their mouths when two policemen walked into the shop. Montana spoke to them, in French.

"Wow," murmured Mouse. "I wish I could speak French like that."

Montana overheard him. "I learned it in school," she told him. "And I have been living in Paris for six years now."

The two policemen asked lots of questions. Montana translated the questions into English and then she told the policemen Mouse and Sam's answers.

At last the two policemen stopped asking things and Montana was able to tell the two children what was happening. "We have two problems," she said. "First, we must get you back with the others from your school, and then we must find Mr Hopkins. The police are going to take us by car across to the Eiffel Tower. You will look and see if your school group is waiting for you there. If they are not there we will take you back to the chateau where you are staying, and the police will make some enquiries about Mr Hopkins. I'm sure he will be all right."

The policemen asked Mouse and Sam what Mr Hopkins' kidnappers looked like. "They were horrible," said Mouse. "They were really big, and had nasty, ugly faces."

"They looked dangerous," Sam added.

They all squeezed into the police car. The policemen didn't want Montana to come, but she insisted. She said that she was going to stay with Sam and Mouse until they were safely back with their school group.

The car sped away from the bookshop with its siren blaring. It was all very exciting. They zoomed over a bridge towards the Eiffel Tower.

"There it is," Montana pointed out.

There were crowds of people milling around the Eiffel Tower. There were school parties everywhere. Mouse thought they would never be able to find anyone. It was like looking for a needle in a haystack.

The policemen led Sam, Mouse and Montana into a lift. "We're going up the Tower so you can look down to the ground for your group," said Montana. They stepped out onto the balcony and looked down.

Suddenly, Sam gave a shout and pointed to the crowds below. "Miss Cherry! Miss Cherry! We've found you!"

Chapter Four

Mr Hopkins the Criminal

Sam and Mouse ran out of the lift. Miss Cherry was looking around with a worried frown on her face. And then the worried look became a small smile, then a big smile, and then a great big smile.

Miss Cherry threw her arms round both the children. "Oh, thank goodness!" she cried. "Where have you been? We waited and waited, and then we decided that you and Mr Hopkins had gone on to the riverside. But you weren't there, so we came on here." Miss Cherry beamed at them and then began wagging her finger. "You wait until I catch up with Mr Hopkins. He's given us such a shock. Where is he?"

Mouse's face fell. At that moment Montana and the two policemen caught up with them.

Montana introduced herself to Miss Cherry and quickly told her the whole story. "We still don't know where Mr Hopkins is," she finished. "But you should be proud of these two. They didn't panic too much. They remembered to use their cards and they found help."

Miss Cherry nodded. "Thank you for looking after them. I know they must have been very worried and scared."

"We ate the best cakes in Paris!" Sam blurted out.

"Hmmm. Maybe you haven't been all that scared then," Miss Cherry said. "However, we still have to find Mr Hopkins. I am very worried about him."

Now that the school party was back together again they left the Eiffel Tower. They had decided that it would be best to go back to the chateau and wait for news about Mr Hopkins.

"He might even be back there waiting for us," Miss Cherry said hopefully.

As they came away from the Tower, Ravi suddenly grabbed Mr Macdonald's arm. "Look!" he cried. "Who's **that?**"

Ravi was pointing at a small poster with a photograph of a man stuck onto a notice board. Mr Macdonald peered at the poster. He shouted to Miss Cherry and Mrs Summerday. Soon, almost everyone was clustered round the notice board, and they were all talking at once.

"What does the writing say?" asked Mrs Summerday. Montana and Mr Macdonald both read the poster carefully.

"It says that this man is wanted by the police," Mr Macdonald told them. "He is one of France's most wanted criminals. He is wanted for bank robberies, a train robbery and murder." Everyone stared again at the photograph on the poster.

"But that's Mr Hopkins," said Jojo, in a tiny voice. And it was. The man on the poster was Mr Hopkins.

Avez-vous vu cet homme?

Recherché pour vol de banque, vol de train et meurtre.

Cheveux:	brun
Yeux:	brun
Taille:	1.75m
Physique:	gros

Si vous voyez cet homme, téléphonez à la police immédiatement.
Il est extrêmement dangereux.

Chapter Five

Miss Cherry's Plan

They stared and stared and stared, but nothing changed. The poster showed Mr Hopkins, and he was wanted for robbery and murder.

"It must be a mistake," said Mrs Summerday.

"It's somebody who looks just like Mr Hopkins," Miss Cherry suggested. "It has to be. I expect that the men who kidnapped him were policemen. They think they have arrested a dangerous criminal."

Mr Macdonald began to laugh quietly. "And instead, they have arrested a harmless primary school teacher. Oh dear!"

The children talked excitedly. Miss Cherry asked them to be quiet. She wanted to get everything sorted out as quickly as possible. She sent Mr Macdonald and Montana to find the policemen who had brought Sam and Mouse to the Eiffel Tower.

When the policemen came back Mr Macdonald and Montana started to explain everything. They showed them the picture on the poster. The policemen were very surprised. They began to nod. They started to smile. One of them burst out laughing. He began talking loudly in French.

"What is he saying?" asked Mrs Summerday.

Montana translated. "He says he thinks it was some friends of his who made the arrest. Mr Hopkins has probably been taken to their headquarters. Now it will be a big joke amongst all the policemen."

Miss Cherry quickly made a plan. "You and Montana go with the police to their headquarters," she told Mr Macdonald. "I will take the children back to the chateau with Mrs Summerday. You can ring me there when you have some news."

So Montana and Mr Macdonald set off to rescue Mr Hopkins, while Miss Cherry and Mrs Summerday went back with the children to the chateau.

Sam and Mouse fell asleep on the coach. Mrs Summerday used their jackets to make blankets so that they stayed warm. "They've had quite an adventure," she said as she sat down beside Miss Cherry.

"Yes, they have," said Miss Cherry. "But I think Mr Hopkins has had even more of an adventure than these two!"

Chapter Six

Safe and Sound

It didn't take long for Mr Macdonald and Montana to sort things out at police headquarters. In fact the police already knew that they had arrested the wrong man.

However, everyone agreed that poor Mr Hopkins did look just like the criminal on the wanted poster. The two policemen who had arrested Mr Hopkins had to put up with a lot of jokes.

"The children who saw you take Mr Hopkins thought you were kidnappers," the policemen's friends told them. "They said that you looked horrible and ugly and dangerous! Ha ha!"

As for Mr Hopkins, he was glad it was all over. "I was just as worried about you lot as I was about myself," he said. "I kept wondering what you would do when you found I was missing."

"But you were not the only one to go missing," said Mr Macdonald. He explained the whole story about Mouse and Sam and Montana.

"I wondered what you were doing here!" said Mr Hopkins, looking at Montana. "Goodness, what a crazy thing to happen."

"Never mind," she said. "It's all over now. We can get back to the others."

Montana offered to drive them back to the chateau. She wanted to make sure that Mouse and Sam were all right. "They were so sensible and brave," she said.

"I think you had a lot to do with that," Mr Macdonald pointed out. "If it hadn't been for your help I don't know what might have happened."

Everyone was very happy to be together again at the chateau. Poor Mr Hopkins had to listen to lots of bad jokes about him being a criminal. Sam and Mouse were delighted to see Montana again, and asked her to stay for supper. Mr Hopkins had two helpings of everything.

"I shall have quite a story to tell when I go back to the bookshop tomorrow morning," Montana said.

"And we shall have quite a story to tell when we get back home," laughed Miss Cherry. "I don't know what our head teacher will say when she finds out that she has a wanted French criminal teaching at our school!"